Time to shed some light on this mystery!

"Wait a minute," she said. "Something else is back here." Bess pointed to something wedged between the floorboards. She knelt down and tugged at it.

"Need a hand?" asked Nancy.

"Nope. I think I've got it," Bess replied. "Here it is." Bess held up a white envelope and stuck it in her pocket. "Okay. Now let's move the dresser back."

The girls leaned against the dresser till it was back against the wall. Then Bess took the envelope out and turned it over. She gasped.

"What is it, Bess?" Nancy asked, worried.

Bess whispered, "The back of this envelope says whatever is inside is top secret."

The Nancy Drew Notebooks

Available from Simon & Schuster

THE
NANCY DREW
NOTEBOOKS®

#60

The Lighthouse Mystery

CAROLYN KEENE
ILLUSTRATED BY PAUL CASALE

Aladdin Paperbacks
New York   London   Toronto   Sydney

First Aladdin Paperbacks edition June 2004
Copyright © 2004 by Simon & Schuster, Inc

ALADDIN PAPERBACKS
An imprint of Simon & Schuster
Children's Publishing Division
1230 Avenue of the Americas
New York, NY 10020

The text of this book was set in Excelsior.

Printed in the United States of America
10 9 8 7 6 5 4 3 2 1

NANCY DREW, THE NANCY DREW NOTEBOOKS, and colophon are registered trademarks of Simon & Schuster, Inc.

Library of Congress Control Number 2003114519

ISBN 0-689-86344-6

1
Road Trip!

What in the world is in that suitcase?" asked eight-year-old Nancy Drew, staring at her best friend, Bess Marvin. "Or, what in the world *isn't* in it?"

Bess was walking toward the Drews' car, pulling a giant suitcase behind her. It was stuffed so full that its zippers were straining. It looked like it would topple over any minute.

Nancy's other best friend, George Fayne, was walking right behind Bess. She didn't have a suitcase at all, just a backpack. "Bess is ready for any emergency," George said. "Especially if it involves her hair."

Bess and George were cousins, but they were very different. George was tall, with dark, curly hair and dark eyes. She loved sports, and she wasn't fussy about the way she looked. Bess was shorter, and blond with blue eyes. Her clothes always matched. She loved headbands and barrettes, cool shoes and jewelry.

"You'll be sorry!" Bess exclaimed. "What if you forgot something? Where we're going it won't be easy to find a new toothbrush. Or sunblock. Or—"

"Just don't ask me to help you get that thing in the car," joked George. "It would take ten strong men to lift it!"

Just then Nancy's dad, Carson Drew, walked out of the garage. "One strong man at least," he agreed, lifting Bess's suitcase into the trunk. "Everybody ready to go?"

"Let me just think for a minute," said Bess. "Do I have everything?"

Nancy and George exchanged a look. Then Nancy said, "We're ready, Dad. Maine, here we come!"

Mr. Drew closed the trunk, and the girls piled into the car. They were taking a road trip! Mr. Drew's old friend Matt Webb had just opened a bed and breakfast on the coast of Maine. The bed and breakfast was in an old lighthouse keeper's house. When Nancy heard her dad planning a trip, she'd asked if she could invite her friends. It *was* summer vacation, after all. And the Webbs had plenty of room in their new inn. Mr. Drew had agreed to bring Bess and George along, and now the girls were crammed into the backseat of the car, sharing a bag of pretzels.

"What should we do first when we get there?" Nancy asked.

"Let's go swimming!" cried George, pumping the air with her fist.

"We could work on our tans," Bess pointed out.

"How about taking a hike?" George countered.

"Or going fishing?" said Mr. Drew. "Maine is famous for its lobsters."

"Ugh! Lobsters!" said Bess with a shudder. "I can't even stand to look at them! All those legs give me the creeps!"

"I wonder if we could climb to the top of

the lighthouse," Nancy said. "I've never been in one before."

"Well," said Mr. Drew, "I wouldn't count on it. Nowadays the lighthouse is run automatically. It doesn't need a keeper anymore—that's why the Webbs were able to turn the keeper's house into a B and B. Someone goes into the lighthouse to check it from time to time, but it's probably not open to everyone."

"That's okay," said Nancy. "I think we'll be pretty busy. Anyone want to play the license plate game? Let's see who can spot plates from all fifty states first."

"I see Massachusetts!" called Bess.

"Me too!" called Nancy.

"There's Nevada!" shouted George. "And look—there's New Jersey! People from everywhere are driving to Maine!"

The girls played the game for a while, and then Mr. Drew put on some music. Later they stopped for gas. Mr. Drew knocked on the window as he was filling the tank, and pointed at the car in front of him in line. "Puerto Rico!" he said, pointing to a license plate. But all three girls were fast asleep.

Nancy woke up first. She'd been asleep for a long time. "Are we there yet?" she asked her father.

"Sure are," he said. "Look at that water!"

Nancy looked out the window and saw the ocean! Waves crashed up on Maine's rocky shore, and Nancy could see boats sailing in the distance. Nancy spotted a long stretch of rock jutting way out into the water. A lighthouse stood at the end of the rocks. Her father caught her eye. "That's the lighthouse, Pudding Pie," he whispered. Nancy woke her friends up right away.

Soon they were at the end of the peninsula, looking up at the lighthouse. "Welcome, Carson!" said a man, stepping out from a white building beside it. He shook Mr. Drew's hand energetically. "This must be Nancy. That strawberry blond hair is just like her mother's!"

Nancy remembered her manners and said, "It's nice to meet you, Mr. Webb. These are my friends, Bess and George."

"It's nice to meet you, too," said Mr. Webb. "And here is my wife, Julia. We are very pleased to have you here with us. Let me take your luggage. Then follow me inside for some dinner!" He lifted Bess's suitcase and hauled it up a flight of stairs to the front door of the white building. Nancy figured it had to be the Webbs' inn.

Inside, a table was set for dinner. Another family was already sitting there, drinking lemonade. "These are our other guests, the Meaneys," said Mr. Webb. "They've come here all the way from Florida."

A girl with short, straight brown hair said, "I'm Megan. I'm in third grade."

A younger girl beside her said almost exactly the same thing. "I'm Hayley. I'm in first grade."

"Hayley is copying me again," Megan reported to her mother.

Before Mrs. Meaney could respond, the Webbs appeared with the food. "Dig in!" said Mrs. Webb. One platter was piled high with ears of corn on the cob. Another was stacked with steaming hamburgers, fresh off the grill. "And be sure to save room for dessert. I've made one of my famous wild-blueberry pies. Or they will be famous, anyway, when the word gets out about our inn."

"This is a beautiful spot," Mr. Drew said to his old friend. "I'm sure there will be a waiting list for guests before the summer's out."

"We hope so," said Mr. Webb. "It's hard to know. We're off the beaten track, as you can see. And the place has a bit of a reputation."

"What kind of reputation?" asked Mr. Drew.

Mr. Webb hesitated. "Well," he said, "a mysterious reputation."

Nancy glanced at her friends. "Mysterious how?" she asked.

"I don't want to scare the kids," said Mr. Webb, looking at Nancy's dad.

"Oh, don't worry about us," Nancy assured him.

Mr. Webb smiled. "It's a long story," he said. "It began a hundred years ago." Mr. Webb gestured toward the window, where the lighthouse was visible. "That's when this lighthouse was built by a local fisherman. Over the years he'd lost too many friends to the sea. So he decided that a lighthouse should go up where so many ships had gone down. He raised the money for it, and built it himself. He was even the first lighthouse keeper. He lived in this very house."

"That doesn't sound mysterious," declared Mr. Drew. "That sounds wonderful. Think of the lives he saved!"

Mr. Webb continued. "But that's just the beginning. The fisherman was lonely in the lighthouse. He missed fishing for a living. Every so often, when there was a clear night with a full moon to guide the ships, he sneaked back to the water. The light-house would be abandoned for a short time, but the fisherman always came back . . . until one night when a storm blew up. That night, a neighbor spotted his boat in the water. But he was never seen or heard from again."

"How awful!" cried Mr. Drew. "What about his family?"

"His family moved away after he vanished," explained Mr. Webb. "But some say the fisherman never left. Since he disappeared, many strange things have happened at the lighthouse. People think the fisherman haunts the place. Everyone around here knows the stories. We just hope they won't scare customers away."

"They won't scare us, that's for sure!" exclaimed George. "Nothing's going to get in the way of our good time here!"

"Unless the ghost does," Bess muttered. "We'd better be careful."

"We come here every summer," said Megan Meaney. "And I've never seen any ghost."

Mrs. Webb agreed. "We hope we *never* see the ghost! Now, would anybody like more pie, or shall I show you to your rooms?"

Soon Nancy, Bess, and George followed Mrs. Webb up to the third floor of the house and down a long hallway. They entered a room with two bunk beds and a slanted ceiling. "I think you'll be comfortable here," said Mrs. Webb. "But ring this bell if you need anything at all."

The girls thanked her and began to unpack their bags.

"What do you think about this ghost?" Bess asked nervously. "Do you guys think it's safe here?"

"Nancy's dad wouldn't bring us here if he thought it was unsafe," George said. "You don't need to be afraid of a ghost. But you might need to be afraid of me!" George leaped at Bess and moaned *"woooooooooo"* until her cousin giggled.

Nancy laughed with her friends. But she couldn't stop thinking about the ghost. Mr. Webb had left out a lot of details. Nancy was wondering about them while Bess and George drifted off to sleep. Finally she drifted off too.

But the next thing she knew, Nancy was wide awake. And there was an eerie bright white light shining in her eyes!

2

Top Secret!

Bess! George!" cried Nancy. "Wake up! Something strange is happening!"

Bess awoke with a start and exclaimed, "The ghost! I knew it!"

Just then, the white light stopped shining. The girls sighed with relief. But then it came back a few minutes later!

"Maybe we should ring for Mrs. Webb," Nancy said.

George jumped out of a bottom bunk and walked bravely to the window. After a quick glance, she said, "Take a look at this." Nancy and Bess drew closer to see what she was looking at. "It's a not a ghost at all,"

12

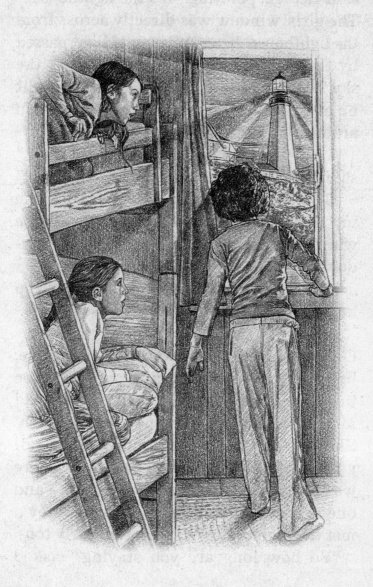

said George, pointing. "It's the lighthouse!" The girls' window was directly across from the lighthouse. Its great beam of light passed by the girls' bedroom as it cut across the sky. The room lit up, then darkened, then lit up again as the light in the lighthouse spun around.

"I can't believe we didn't notice it before," said Nancy, a little embarrassed.

"The blinds were closed when we came in," Bess explained. "I opened them a little while ago when I got up to open the window."

George yawned. "Can we go back to sleep now? I want to get up early for a swim!"

George's alarm clock went off at sunrise, but the girls weren't the first ones up at the inn. "We always get an early start," said Mrs. Webb, folding napkins in the kitchen. She set some homemade muffins and tall glasses of orange juice on the table. There was a place set for each of the girls—and one set for Megan Meaney, the girl they'd met the night before. She was up early too.

"So how long are you staying?" asked

Megan, breaking a muffin in two. "My family will be here for a whole week."

"Just a few days," said Nancy.

"That's not nearly enough time to do everything," Megan replied. "Trust me—my family comes here every summer."

"Maybe you can tell us the best place to go swimming, then," said George. "The beach here looks a little rocky."

"Most beaches in Maine *are* rocky," Megan said importantly. "A beach with sand is something special here. But don't worry—*I* know where to find one. Abigail showed me."

"Abigail?" asked Nancy. "I thought your sister's name was Hayley."

"Hayley *is* my sister," said Megan. "Abigail is my friend. She lived in this house until the Webbs bought it last winter. I met her one summer when we were really little, and I've seen her every summer after that."

"It must be weird to stay in her house now that it's not her house anymore," said George.

"It is pretty weird," Megan agreed. "My family usually stays in a hotel, but my parents thought it would be exciting to stay

15

closer to the lighthouse this year. They haven't been inside the lighthouse, but I have—loads of times. Abigail's dad was the last lighthouse keeper here."

"Wow!" cried Nancy. "How did you get up there? What was it like?"

"Oh, Abigail could go up whenever she wanted," Megan said. "And it was really cool. You could see for miles from up there."

"You weren't scared of ghosts, or anything?" ventured Bess.

"Of the fisherman's ghost? Oh, nobody really believes those stories." Megan dismissed them with a wave of her hand. "And if there was a ghost, Abigail probably knew him. She knew this place like the back of her hand. She showed me the best place to get ice cream—a place only the locals know. She introduced me to the coolest people in town. She taught me how to sail—and you should see me now!"

"You must really miss her," Nancy said.

"Yeah. This year Abigail's gone and all that's left is a bunch of tourists. . . . I mean, no offense," Megan stumbled, "but it just isn't the same."

"It just isn't the same," mimicked a voice in the doorway. It was Megan's little sister, Hayley. "*Nobody* is as cool as Abigail!" she said in a mocking tone.

"Oh, leave me alone, Hayley," groaned Megan. "Can't I say anything without you saying it again?"

"Oh, leave me alone," Hayley repeated. She poured herself a glass of juice.

Megan glared at her sister. To break the silence, George said, "So where's that beach you mentioned, Megan? Are you up for a swim?"

Megan and Hayley suddenly agreed on something. "It's pretty cold," said Megan.

"It's *freezing*," Hayley added. "We go swimming at home in Florida. Here we stay out of the water."

"But I know the best place to go, of course," Megan continued. "Walk back to Maine Street. Then make a left. You'll pass the general store and come to a blue house. There's a private beach behind the house, but the people who live there let anybody use it. Anybody who knows about it, that is. Tell them Megan sent you."

"Thanks, Megan!" cried Nancy.

"See you later!" called George as she bounded up the stairs.

Bess closed the door behind her friends once they were all back in their room. "It's not that I don't like her, okay? But what did she mean by 'tourists'? Isn't she a tourist too? And I'm sure *somebody* believes in the lighthouse ghost. I'm *glad* she doesn't want to swim with us!"

"And what was with her sister?" George asked.

Nancy shrugged.

Bess was digging through her suitcase. "Oh, where did I put my bathing suit? Maybe I did pack too much stuff. . . ."

Bess began to pile things on the dresser near her bunk bed: a stack of socks, a bottle of shampoo, and a curling iron. "Is that a curling iron?" asked George, surprised.

"For emergencies," Bess said, hiding it under some T-shirts.

Nancy and George both laughed as Bess kept hunting for her bathing suit. "Oh, there it is!" she cried. "And . . . oh, no!" Some of Bess's things had fallen behind the dresser. "Can one of you help me get the shampoo out from behind there?"

George took one side of the dresser, and Nancy took the other. "One, two, three, push!" Nancy counted. The girls shoved the dresser a few feet away from the wall. Bess crept behind it and located her bottle of shampoo.

"Wait a minute," she said. "Something else is back here." Bess pointed to something wedged between the floorboards. She knelt down and tugged at it.

"Need a hand?" asked Nancy.

"Nope. I think I've got it," Bess replied. "Here it is." Bess held up a white envelope and stuck it in her pocket. "Okay. Now let's move the dresser back."

The girls leaned against the dresser till it was back against the wall. Then Bess took the envelope out and turned it over. She gasped.

"What is it, Bess?" Nancy asked, worried.

Bess whispered, "The back of this envelope says whatever is inside is top secret."

3

A Puzzling Puzzle

Do you think we should open it?" Bess asked.

"Of course we should open it!" cried George, looking to Nancy for backup.

"I think we should too. We'll need to decide whether to tell the Webbs," Nancy said.

Bess ripped the envelope open. A jigsaw puzzle piece and a bit of folded paper fell to the floor. The girls knelt to look at the mysterious objects. The puzzle piece was small and red. On the paper someone had pasted cut-out letters that spelled out the words: "Puzzled? Pieces on land and sea will lead you to the key."

"Can I see the envelope again?" Nancy asked. Bess passed it to her friend. Nancy stuck her hand inside the envelope and pulled out a small sketched map wedged inside. "Maybe this will help us," Nancy said.

"But help us do *what*?" George questioned.

"Find something?" Nancy guessed.

Bess said, "Like . . . ?"

Just then a voice outside their door said, "Wait for me, Hayley!"

"Oh no," whispered George. "Megan Meaney."

"Let's go to the beach as we planned," suggested Bess. "I don't want to show her this stuff."

The three girls changed quickly and packed a few things for their outing. Nancy stashed the torn envelope and its contents in her backpack. When the girls left their room and spotted Megan at the end of the hall, they waved as if nothing was up. They left a note to tell Nancy's dad where they'd gone.

Outside, Nancy and her friends followed the path Megan had described for them. "Look, there's the ice cream place," Bess pointed out. "We'll have to go there later."

"And here's the blue house," said George. When they walked around to the back, the girls spotted an elderly couple in rocking chairs on the porch, looking at the water. "Megan sent us!" George called to the couple.

The woman said, "Who?"

"Megan Meaney! Abigail's friend!" George explained.

And the woman replied, "Oh, Abigail! We miss her dearly. Enjoy the beach!"

The beach was on a small cove with a rock jetty on either side. Past one jetty, the girls noticed some boats docked. The blue water stretched as far as they could see, and the lighthouse shone brightly in the distance. It was a beautiful spot.

George spread out a beach towel and Bess put on some sunscreen. Nancy took the envelope from her backpack. "Ready to take a closer look?" she asked her friends. Nancy unzipped a secret compartment in her backpack and removed two things she used for solving mysteries: her magnifying glass and the special blue notebook her father had given her for writing down clues.

First Nancy looked at the note with her glass. "These letters must be from a news-paper—they're definitely on newsprint," she observed. "But the paper isn't that old."

"How do you know?" Bess asked.

"Because when newspaper is old, it turns yellow, and this paper is only a little yellow."

Next Nancy turned to the map. It was drawn by hand, and not drawn very well. Nancy studied the map for minute. *What could this map be a picture of?* she thought to herself. Suddenly she had an idea. "Oh, look!" she said. "Doesn't this map remind you of the area around the lighthouse?"

George was good with maps and direc-tions. She leaned over to look more closely. "Hey, I think you might be right!" she said. "Here's the lighthouse. Here's the Webbs' B and B. Here's Maine Street and the blue house. Here's the beach we're on!"

"That's what I was afraid of," said Nancy mysteriously.

"Wait," said Bess. "Can we back up for a minute? We have a map that is supposed to help us find something. But what do you think it is?"

Nancy took out her notebook and opened it to a fresh page. Then she uncapped a pen and wrote, "The Case of the Lighthouse Secret." "We don't know exactly what we're looking for," Nancy admitted. "But we do know that this is a mystery—and somebody wants us to solve it!"

"The note says we'll find the *key*. That must mean the key to this mystery," George said. "Maybe things will be clear when we find it. And we have three clues to go on already."

"The puzzle piece, the note, and the map," Bess said. "I'm with you so far."

George looked at the note again. "Pieces at land and sea . . . ," she read. " I wonder if that could mean more puzzle pieces."

Nancy nodded. "That's what I think. If we find more puzzle pieces, we can put them together—and find the key to this mystery."

Bess sighed. "But where will we find them? We don't even know where to start."

"That's where the map comes in," Nancy said cheerfully, handing it to Bess. "See those small X's? We should look in those places first. But that's the confusing part." Nancy pointed to the map and said, "If the lighthouse is here, and we are here, the X's will be pretty hard to get to."

"You're right," Bess said. She looked around to get her bearings. "One X is in the water and one is on the rocks. Not so handy," she said with a sigh. "I thought this was supposed to be a vacation," Bess said. "How about we take a vacation from solving mysteries?"

Nancy shook her head. "What kind of detectives walk away from a mystery just because they're at the beach?"

Bess sank back down onto her towel. Nancy looked at her friend and said, "But let's collect some seashells before we do anything else."

The three girls walked to the water's edge. It was as cold as Megan Meaney had promised. Nancy, George, and Bess waded along the edge of the water, collecting shells and sea glass.

"I found a sand dollar!" Nancy said as a seagull squawked overhead.

George nodded toward the blue house and said, "Did you guys think it was weird that the people who own this beach didn't know Megan? They acted like they'd never heard of her."

"They probably hadn't," Bess said. "Megan thinks she knows everything, but without Abigail, she'd just be a tourist—like us."

Nancy didn't respond. She didn't think Megan was so bad.

Luckily the girls had just come to one of the rock jetties. The sand at the base of it was covered in stones and shells. The girls filled their pockets with more beach treasures, then Bess clambered up on the jetty to look around. She reported to her friends: "Lots of boats are coming in!"

George climbed up beside her. "I hate to say it, Bess, but I think those are lobster boats." She made her hand into a claw and pretended to pinch her cousin. But Bess didn't see it. She was busy staring out into the water.

Bess said, "I just thought of something. Let's take another look at that map, okay?"

The girls headed back to their towels,

and Nancy pulled out the map. Bess pointed to it and said, "See that X there? The one that looks like it's *in* the water? What if it's *on* the water instead? Maybe it's on a boat?"

Nancy looked at the map from a different angle. "I think you could be right," she agreed, placing a finger on the map. "If this spot is the beach, that spot is where the docks are."

"Maybe our next clue is right there!" exclaimed George. She pointed to the dock where lots of boats were tied.

The boats were full of lobstermen stacking traps and cleaning up. "I don't think this is a good time for us to be looking around," Nancy pointed out. "But why don't we come back when the boats are empty?"

Since that wouldn't be till evening, the girls took a long walk around the village. Later they had dinner at the inn. As she cleared plates Nancy asked her dad if he wanted to go for a walk on the beach.

"Matt and I were just thinking the same thing," said Mr. Drew. "But let's go soon so we're back before dark."

Nancy ran upstairs to get her backpack.

The note, the puzzle pieces, and the map were all stored inside. But when she got to the room she stopped in her tracks.

Her backpack was gone!

4

The Floating Clue

When Nancy came back downstairs, she acted like everything was normal. She wanted to wait until she could be alone with her friends. But George and Bess could tell something was wrong. "What's up?" George whispered when she thought nobody else could hear.

"My backpack!" Nancy whispered back. "It's gone!"

She didn't realize that Hayley was standing behind her. "You left it on the deck," she announced. "I hung it on one of the pegs near the door." Hayley looked curiously at Nancy. "Did you think someone had taken it?"

"No . . . I just wouldn't want to lose it, that's all," Nancy stammered.

I don't remember leaving my backpack there, Nancy thought as she left with the others for a walk.

Mr. Drew and Mr. Webb walked way ahead of the girls, lost in conversation. "They're probably telling old stories," Nancy told her friends. "Now we can search for clues!"

When they came to the beach, Nancy waved at her dad and motioned to the other side of the jetty. "We're going over there for a minute," Nancy called.

The girls climbed over the jetty and found themselves on a rockier beach. Three docks extended from the rocks into the deep water.

"Okay, we're here. Now what?" said George. The girls walked along one of the docks until they came to several boats.

Nancy looked at the map. "The X is in the middle of this area, and we are on the middle dock. Maybe we should try one of the boats that's tied up right here?"

George was looking at the boats in front of them. "Hey! Look!" she said. "This one's called the *Abigail*. At least we know the name. Maybe this is a good one to start with."

"Let's go and see!" said Nancy.

"We're really going on board?" Bess asked. "Are you sure that's a good idea?"

"It's just for a minute," George reassured her.

"And my dad is right over there—if anything goes wrong, we can yell," Nancy added. "We just need to see if there's any place a puzzle piece might be hidden. That's the only way we'll know if your hunch is right."

Bess didn't argue. George climbed aboard the *Abigail*, then helped her friends on after her. The boat swayed with the waves and Nancy almost lost her footing.

A pile of lobster traps was in a corner of the deck. Near it was a heap of buoys, a tangle of rope, and some other gear. Nancy and George poked around the pile. Bess gingerly opened a lobster trap and peered inside. The girls didn't notice anything unusual.

George straightened up and said, "I don't think we're going to find anything on deck."

"Maybe we should look in here," Nancy

suggested. She pointed at the glassed-in cabin where the boat's controls were. She opened the door and walked in.

George sat at the wheel and pretended to steer the boat for a minute. Then she turned to her right. "Check this out!" she said. Nancy and Bess ran over. George had found some low shelves where odds and ends were stored. On one shelf were two books of crossword puzzles. "Whoever sails this boat likes puzzles," George said.

"Maybe we're getting warmer," said Nancy.

Bess held one puzzle book upside down and shook it, but nothing fell out. George turned the pages of the other to see if it contained a clue. She had no luck either.

Nancy sat down on a tackle box by the door to the cabin. Just then the next wave rocked the boat and tossed her to the floor! "Uh-oh," said Nancy. "I don't think I have my sea legs yet." As she turned the box right side up, Nancy heard a rattle. She opened the box and found it full of puzzle pieces. "Somebody around here must *really* like puzzles. It's got to be hard to do a jigsaw on a boat!"

"Could our clue be in the picture?" Bess wondered.

"Let's put it together and see," said George. The girls assembled the small puzzle on the driver's seat. It pictured a lighthouse on a sunny day. The scene was perfect and no pieces were out of place. "I think we're out of luck," said Nancy. "Maybe we should head back."

"Wait a minute!" said Bess. "Here's another tackle box." She gave it a shake. "Sounds like something's inside this one too." Bess undid the latch—and found a lone puzzle piece!

It was red, like the first piece, and about the same size. But it had a hole drilled in the middle and a chain through the hole. It looked like a puzzle piece necklace.

"I don't get the necklace part," said George. "But let's see if it fits the other piece."

Nancy drew the original piece from her backpack and put it together with the one Bess had found. It fit perfectly! "One piece down, one to go," Nancy announced, putting the new piece around her neck. She tucked it under her shirt and said, "Can't be too safe. Until we know what the 'key' is, I think we should keep the mystery to ourselves." She paused, then added, "We'd better get going. My dad will be worried."

As the whole group headed back to the B and B, the girls had a chance to talk about their case some more. "I guess the next clue will be on land," said George. "But if we follow the map to that other X we'll land on a pile of rocks!"

"Let's look at the map again when we get back," Nancy said. "Maybe it will shed some more light on the mystery now that we've found a new clue." She paused, then added, "Speaking of light, look at the moon!"

A full moon was rising over the beach. The sky was growing darker, but the girls could see their way clearly by the moon's bright light.

Bess drew in her breath. "A full moon!" she whispered dramatically. "You know what that means!"

"No. What?" asked her cousin.

"The fisherman's ghost could come out tonight!" Bess reminded her.

"I don't think we need to worry," Nancy soothed her friend. "We're not going anywhere."

"Just to our room," said Bess, "which is right across from the lighthouse. That's ghost central! Maybe one of us should keep a lookout."

"That's right!" exclaimed George. "Look out!" She began to chase Bess toward the lighthouse. Bess ran as fast as she could, looking back from time to time to make sure no ghost was behind her. Nancy kept up with her friends, and the three arrived breathless at the B and B.

The Meaneys were on the deck. Mr. Meaney was taking pictures of the bright purple sky. Hayley was painting her toenails. Megan was nowhere to be seen.

Nancy went upstairs to put away her sleuthing gear. On her way back down, she ran into Megan Meaney. Megan was carrying a video and said, "Mrs. Webb will let us watch this in the living room. Want to come?"

Then she stopped and stared at Nancy. At first Nancy thought Megan was looking at her hair, which was wild and messy from her run to the inn. Then she realized Megan was looking at her neck. Nancy reached up, but it was too late. The puzzle necklace had flown out, and Megan Meaney had spotted it. Megan said, "Nancy, why are you wearing Abigail's necklace?"

5

Detective Meaney?

Nancy didn't like to lie. But she didn't know what to say. Luckily her friends had just come up the stairs. She hoped they could help.

"That's not Abigail's necklace," said Bess. "Nancy's had it for . . . forever."

"Or at least since her birthday," George corrected. "I, um, gave it to her."

Megan came closer. She lifted up the necklace, and took a good look. "I don't think so," she said. "I've seen this necklace before. Abigail's oldest brother gave it to her one Christmas—both of them loved puzzles." Megan pointed to a small scratch

on the back of the puzzle piece. Nancy hadn't noticed it before. "See that?" Megan asked. "Abigail got that scratch on the necklace last summer."

Megan glared at the girls. "Are you going to tell me where you got it?"

Now Bess and George were tongue-tied. So Nancy did the only thing she could do: She told the truth. Megan seemed surprised when she heard about the note. "Well, you're staying in Abigail's old room," she said. "And now you've found Abigail's necklace. Maybe Abigail wrote the note and hid it behind her dresser."

"Hmm," said Nancy. "I hadn't thought of that."

"See?" said Megan. "I'm a detective too! How about I help you guys look for the next clue? After all, I know my way around. I can think of a million places to hide more clues. You need me on your case!"

All of a sudden, Bess could speak again. "Oh, we solve mysteries on our own all the time," she said.

Nancy glanced at her friends, then turned to Megan and said, "We'll show you the

41

map after the movie. We're trying to keep a low profile, you know."

Megan winked and said, "Meet you upstairs."

The girls settled into the Webbs' living room to watch the video with Hayley. Nancy had seen the movie before, but she kept quiet while the others watched. Megan, on the other hand, talked through the whole thing. "This is my favorite part!" she shouted, pointing at the screen. "Wait till you see what happens next!"

"Do you mind?" said Hayley. "Some of us want to *hear* what happens too."

Megan paused the movie for a second and said, "Some of us know something you don't know, Hayley." Megan looked meaningfully at Nancy, who looked the other way. She didn't want to start a fight. Megan and her sister seemed to argue all the time.

Nancy went back to her room before the movie was over. Bess and George arrived a little later. Now they were just waiting for Megan.

Bess flopped on a bottom bunk and said, "How could you tell her?"

Nancy shook her head. "I'm sorry!" she said. Nancy had been looking at the map, which she showed to her friends again. "I just can't figure out how we'll find this next clue. We got lucky the last time, but this time we need some help. And Megan really does know her way around."

George threw up her hands, and Bess looked at the floor. Nancy took their silence as a good sign. She reached for her notebook, traced the shape of the puzzle necklace into it, and wrote "Abigail's necklace."

"So Abigail left that note," Bess said as if nothing had happened. "But why? What kind of secret could she have?"

"Maybe Megan knows," George replied. "That's one good reason to have her on our team."

Nancy smiled. Just then there was a knock at the door, and Megan Meaney walked into the room.

"Here I am. I don't think I've been followed," she whispered, laughing. "When do I get to see the map?"

Nancy unfolded it again and showed it to Megan. "Here's where we found the first puzzle piece," she explained, pointing to the X near the docks.

Megan began talking. "You went on the *Abigail*, right? How did you like it? That's Abigail's brother's boat. He used to take us out in it all the time. We'd do puzzles if the water was calm. He still lives around here."

Nancy tried to keep Megan on the subject. "The boat was nice," she said. "Now, here's where the next clue could be." She pointed to the X near the base of the lighthouse. Even Megan was stumped for a minute.

"It'll be like looking for a needle in a haystack," she said.

"Did you ever go down there with Abigail?" Bess prompted her.

Megan brightened up. "Actually, yes, I did. We had the best time! We packed a picnic and rode our bikes to the end of the peninsula. Then we hiked down the rocks to a bunch of caves at the water line. Abigail said nobody knew they were there. Then later we were going to go up in the lighthouse, but . . ."

"Well, that would make perfect sense," George jumped in. "We need to check the caves. Abigail would hide her clues in places she knows."

Bess looked at Megan and asked, "What do you think Abigail could be hiding?"

Megan shrugged. "I have no clue," she said. "She tells me everything."

Now Nancy had a question. "What has she said about her new home? Maybe she's given you some clues that you didn't pick up on."

Megan shifted in her seat. "I haven't talked to her in a while," she said.

"Did she move far away?" asked Nancy.

"Not too far. Just to Boston," Megan answered. "She's just been really busy. I know *I* have," she said. Then she changed the subject. "Did I tell you I'm on the gymnastics team?"

Nancy listened politely, then said, "Do you think you could show us the caves tomorrow?"

"Sure," said Megan. "I'd love to show you around." But before the girls could make a plan, there was a faint scratching sound in the hallway.

"What's that?" asked Nancy sharply.

"I'm sure no one's out there," said Megan.

"All the grown-ups have gone to bed. And who would bother to spy on us, anyway?"

Bess pursed her lips and said, "Detectives just like to keep their business to themselves, if you know what I mean."

Suddenly all the lights in the room began to flicker on and off. They wouldn't stop! Megan tried to explain. "Oh, this happens all the time here. Old houses, you know."

But George wasn't convinced. She went to the window. "The lighthouse light is on," she reported. "But I don't think that's what is flickering. . . ."

"And everyone's in bed but us?" Bess asked in a shaky voice. "I don't like the sound of that."

Megan tried to make a joke out of it, but Nancy could tell she was getting nervous. "So the lights are flashing," she said. "What do we need them for, anyway? We're about to go to bed."

"Maybe you are," retorted Bess. "But I can't go to sleep knowing what's out there!"

George was confused. "But we *don't* know what's out there."

"Oh, yes we do," cried Bess. "It's the ghost!"

6

Clue in a Cave

T he ghost!" giggled Megan. "You don't really believe that, do you?"

Bess sat up straight and said, "I sure do!"

Nancy stepped in quickly. "There has to be some other explanation. Nobody even knows for sure if there *is* a ghost."

The noise in the hallway stopped as suddenly as it had begun. Then the lights stopped flashing too. Bess sighed with relief.

Megan turned to Nancy and said, "I'll see you guys tomorrow. Unless the ghost catches me on my way back to my room." With that, she flounced out the door.

"She sure talks a lot," Bess said once Megan was safely out of earshot.

"Yeah," said George. "Do we really need her help?"

Nancy answered. "Megan might not be easy to get along with. But I still think she might help us find the 'key'—whatever it is."

The next day was gray and gloomy. At breakfast Mr. Webb said, "It wouldn't be summer in Maine without a rainy day!" He opened a closet full of board games, and the guests played Monopoly for most of the morning. The rain had stopped by the afternoon, though, and the girls were getting restless. Nancy was glad to hear Megan say, "Do you want to take a walk down by the water?"

Hayley shuddered and said, "Isn't it a little cold?" But Nancy knew what Megan meant. Together, they'd try to find the next clue.

The girls put on their sweatshirts, and Megan led the way past the lighthouse to the end of the rocky peninsula. "Watch your step," she ordered. "It's slippery." The girls climbed down carefully and found themselves beneath a cliff. In front of them waves crashed onto the sand. Behind them were two small caves.

Megan pointed at one of them. "Abigail played hide-and-seek here with her brothers."

Nancy took a flashlight out of her backpack and shone it on the inside walls. They were smooth and wet. "There aren't many places to hide things," she pointed out. "And anything hidden would be washed away by the tide."

The next cave was more promising, though. "This one is narrower," said Nancy, "and it stretches way back under the bluff. Some of it probably stays dry."

Nancy ran her fingers along the cave walls, searching for anything that might be in the crevices. Bess tried to crawl into the back of the cave, but the space was too small for her. "I'll go!" said George. She had no problem shimmying in.

"There's a sign back here," she shouted out to her friends. "It says ABIGAIL'S HIDE-OUT! I think we're in the right place."

Megan frowned at Nancy and Bess. "Hide-out?" she said. "Abigail never showed me that part of the cave."

"Can you hand me the flashlight?" George asked. Nancy held it through the opening. Suddenly George reappeared, holding a treasure chest. She said, "Let's open it up!"

Nancy lifted the lid. The inside was lined with gold fabric. Another red puzzle piece was nestled right in the middle!

Nancy was looking for the other pieces in her backpack when she heard someone laughing. "What's so funny?" she asked, lifting her head. None of the other girls were laughing. Instead they were staring at the other cave opening, where the noise seemed to come from. The laugh was an eerie cackle.

"Sounds like the ghost to me," Bess said, shivering.

"I'm sure it's not a ghost," insisted Megan. But she didn't seem as sure as she had the night before.

"What are we going to do?" Bess wailed. "I hear something else, too! A thunderstorm!"

"We need to stay calm," Nancy said. "Ghost or no ghost, my dad told me it's not

50

safe for us to be on the beach in a storm. He said to find shelter and wait it out." The girls trembled as the cave grew colder and darker. The cave was lit with flashes of lightning. Thunder rumbled in the distance.

Nancy thought she heard someone calling her name as the girls waited out the storm. It sounded like her dad! But when Nancy called back, her voice didn't carry far. Nobody came to rescue them.

"I think the storm is moving away," George said after a while. "Hear how there's more time between the light and the sound?"

Eventually things seemed a little less frightening. And then the rain stopped too. As they walked back to the B and B, Bess said, "Did you notice that the ghost stopped laughing when the storm started?"

"Maybe he was rained out," Megan said meanly.

Even Nancy was a little tired of Megan after the afternoon's adventures. Luckily the Meaneys were waiting for her at the inn—the whole family was going out to dinner. Nancy and her friends would be on their own.

When they returned to the B and B, Mr. Drew and the Webbs were busy cooking. "Thank goodness you're all right!" Mr. Drew exclaimed.

"We were safe in a cave, Daddy. We hid just like you said," Nancy said, giving her dad a hug. Then Nancy and her friends went out to the deck. The girls put together the three pieces of the puzzle. Together they made a red octagon. There were no more clues, just a faint dot toward one of the puzzle's edges.

"Not much of a key," Bess said wryly.

"Could it be one more clue?" Nancy wondered.

"The key to the key?" George said. "Maybe."

"I'm stumped," said Nancy. "We've followed the map, but we have no idea where to go next. I thought that Megan might help us understand what Abigail was up to, but she hasn't helped much at all."

Bess and George glanced at each other.

Nancy sounded discouraged. "We're at a dead end."

Bess and George were discouraged for a moment too.

Then Bess said, "Someone else doesn't want us to find out the secret, whatever it is."

"What do you mean?" asked George and Nancy at the same time.

"Every time we work on the case, something strange happens."

"You mean the ghost shows up?" George said with a grin.

Bess looked very serious. "That's what I think. Don't laugh."

"Couldn't it be a coincidence?" Nancy asked.

Bess frowned. "It could be," she answered slowly.

Nancy changed the subject. "How about we take a bike ride tomorrow? Mr. and Mrs. Webb said they have extra kids' bikes in the garage," she said. "We might not solve the mystery, but at least we'll have fun on our own."

"Sounds like a plan," said George. "Now let's go inside and eat!"

The girls had chicken and potato salad with Mr. Drew and the Webbs. Afterward they helped clear the table. "So how do you girls like staying on the third floor?" asked Mrs. Webb. "We think we'll use your bedroom for kids whenever they come to stay."

"We love it!" said Nancy. "We love everything about this place." Bess didn't mention the ghost.

"Too bad you won't be here this weekend," said Mrs. Webb. "The Coast Guard is coming to make some repairs to the lighthouse, and it will be open for a couple of days."

"Oh, I wish we could go to the top!" Nancy said.

"You'll just have to come back sometime!" Mrs. Webb said, smiling. "Abigail told me the lighthouse was the best place in the world for kids to play."

Nancy looked up from the plate she was scraping. "I didn't know you knew Abigail!" she replied. "We've heard a lot about her."

Mrs. Webb explained, "I met Abigail a few times when we were looking at the house. She was very sad to be moving. She really loved the lighthouse."

"We heard that too," George mentioned casually. "We heard that Abigail knew lots of secrets about the place." She winked at Nancy, but nobody else could see.

"Come to think of it," said Mrs. Webb, "Abigail did seem to know some secrets. She said something mysterious about how she wouldn't be the last kid to have a sleepover at the top of the lighthouse. Of course that would never be allowed! But she seemed convinced."

"What did she mean?" Nancy asked. "How could that be?"

Mrs. Webb shook her head. "Your guess is as good as mine. But Abigail seemed positive there would be a way."

7

A New Twist

Nancy couldn't wait to be done with the dishes. She wanted to discuss this latest development with her friends. Nancy dried and stacked the plates so perfectly that Mrs. Webb said, "Want a job at the inn? You're hired!"

As the girls headed out of the kitchen, Nancy whispered, "We need to have a meeting, and I know just where it should be." Nancy asked her dad if they could to go to the ice-cream parlor. Soon the girls were sitting on a bench outside, eating cones with chocolate sprinkles for dessert.

"Abigail's secret *has* to have something

to do with what Mrs. Webb said," Nancy announced. "Something to do with sleep-overs in the lighthouse."

"That's the last place I'd want to have a sleepover!" Bess exclaimed. "It's haunted! *I* think that Abigail's secret has something to do with the ghost. Why else would he keep getting in our way? Maybe Abigail knew something about him—and he doesn't want it getting out."

"Maybe," said Nancy, unconvinced.

"Maybe," agreed George. "But let's get back to what Mrs. Webb said."

"Abigail left her note in the kids' bedroom," said Nancy. "I think she wanted a kid to find it. Somehow Abigail's secret will let kids play in the lighthouse again."

"But it doesn't make sense," George pointed out. "Kids can't get into the lighthouse. Nobody can."

"Maybe there's a secret entrance or something. I don't know." Nancy polished off the last of her cone.

"Here's what I'm wondering," Bess blurted out. "How come Megan never told us Abigail knew a way kids could sleep over there?

She's supposed to be helping us with the mystery. Is she trying to stop us instead?"

"I'm sure she wouldn't do that," said Nancy. "Maybe she just didn't know."

"But why wouldn't she know? Abigail is her best friend," Bess reminded Nancy.

"Maybe Abigail never told her!" George cried. "Don't you think it's weird that they haven't talked in a long time? And that Megan didn't know about the hideout? Maybe they're not as close as Megan says."

"Let's take another look at the puzzle pieces," Nancy said. "They're all we have to go on."

Nancy unzipped her backpack and took out the octagon. While her friends were looking at it, Nancy jotted a few more things in her notebook: "Second piece found in cave" and "Abigail's secret sleepovers?"

Bess nudged Nancy as she was tracing the shape of the octagon onto a blank page. "Remember how you said we were at a dead end? Maybe we're not, after all! Doesn't this shape remind you of a stop sign? Could the answer be near one?"

"It could be!" Nancy said excitedly. "It's

the best lead we've had in a while! It won't be dark for a while yet—let's look around."

The girls walked from the ice cream parlor to the downtown area of Maine Street. It didn't take them long to locate the two stop signs in town.

George found one at the main intersection, where a larger town might have had a traffic light. Standing beneath it, she looked in all directions. But all she saw were a telephone pole, a flock of seagulls, and a T-shirt shop that was closing up. None of them seemed connected to Abigail's secret.

Nancy and Bess investigated the other stop sign. It was at the end of the shopping district, where Maine Street became just like any other sleepy street in town. This one was leaning a little toward the water. It didn't seem to offer any clues either.

The girls stood beneath it until Nancy said, "Let's take a break." They met up with George, walked down toward the water, and watched the tide go out.

Behind them, people walked down Maine Street. "The sun is going down!" said a voice. "Take a picture of the lighthouse!"

Nancy wished she had her camera. She would have liked her own picture of the lighthouse. Instead, she opened her notebook and started to draw a picture. Since there were no more clues, she'd at least make a record of what she'd seen on her vacation. As she started to draw it, though, Nancy realized something. The lighthouse had eight sides, like a stop sign. It was octagonal. Could the final clue be there?

Nancy couldn't contain herself. "I think I've got it!" she shouted to her friends. "We have to go to the lighthouse!"

Bess and George jumped up and they all headed down the rocky peninsula. Before they got too far, though, they heard another voice. This one said, "You guys are going to the lighthouse? What for?"

It was Megan Meaney, with her whole family. They were coming back from the restaurant where they'd had dinner.

There was no point in lying—Megan already knew they were looking for something. "I think we're going to get to the bottom of our mystery!" Nancy said.

Megan bragged about how well she knew

the lighthouse. "I used to go there all the time with Abigail," she said.

"You used to do everything with Abigail!" Hayley interrupted. "I'm glad she's not here this year."

Megan ignored her sister. "I think I know a way in. Follow me!"

Nancy motioned George and Bess to follow too. Mr. and Mrs. Meaney continued to the Webbs', but Hayley hung back.

Megan never seemed nice to Hayley, and she wasn't nice now. "Hayley, you can't come with us! This mission is for detectives only!"

Nancy didn't want to have to explain everything to Hayley. But she felt sorry for the younger girl. She said, "Hayley, would you mind telling my dad where we are? I don't want him to wonder. We'll be back really soon."

Hayley nodded and left without a word. Megan led the girls around the back of the lighthouse. There was no door there, just a workman's ladder that led to a small window near the ground. Megan said, "You can go right up the stairs once you get through the window."

Nancy and her friends climbed up the ladder and through the window one by one. And as they entered the lighthouse, a low moan began in the distance.

8

The Haunted Lighthouse

The inside of the lighthouse was dark and very narrow. Once they climbed through the window, the girls were on a landing between two flights of winding stairs. Megan led the way up. The stairs wound to the right, and it seemed like they would never end. Every so often, the girls came to another landing with a window. Through the window they could see the darkening sky. They could also hear the faint sound of the moaning below.

Nancy knew Bess thought it was the ghost. Right now Nancy couldn't think of a better explanation. So she decided not to think about it at all.

Finally Megan stopped. "We're here!" she yelled. The top of the lighthouse was a small room lined with more windows. Nancy could see the B and B far below, and waves smashing against the rocks. But there was no time to admire the view.

"What are we looking for, exactly?" Megan asked.

"That's the problem," Nancy explained. "We're still not sure." Then she had a great idea. "Would you mind keeping guard while we search?" she asked. Nancy didn't know what Megan could guard them from. But at least the job would keep her out of the way.

George walked around the room, checking the walls for any openings where something might be hidden. Bess stuck with Nancy, walking toward the huge light in the middle of the room. Nancy saw spots after she'd looked at the light for a moment. There was no way Abigail would have hidden her secret there.

Nancy had left the red octagon in her pocket. She took it out again and noticed something new. The faint spot was in the middle of one of the eight sides. And an even fainter *N* was below it! "Look at this," she said to Bess. But Bess was too scared to pay attention to anything but the strange noises in the distance.

Nancy showed George instead, and George thought fast. "What if it's *N* for north, like on a map? Where's the north side of the lighthouse?"

The girls knew the sun was in the west now. Working from there, they found the north side and did a search. Nancy ran her hand along the base of one of the windows, and suddenly she felt something sticking out!

Nancy looked closely and grabbed hold of something red. She pulled on it until it broke free of the window. It was another red octagon. And this one had a string attached. Nancy tugged and tugged on the string until she pulled out . . . a key!

"Of course!" cried Nancy. "'Pieces on land and sea will lead you to the key!' I can't believe I didn't think of that! But what will it open?"

George said, "Could it be a key to the lighthouse? Let's go downstairs and try!"

The girls had to slip past Megan to get back to the stairs. Megan let them by without a word. She stayed at her guard post—and Bess needed a guard by now, she was so upset about what she could hear. "Don't go down there!" she said, quivering. "The ghost is at the bottom of the stairs!"

Nancy couldn't push Bess's worries from her mind any longer. The awful sound did seem to be right outside the door. Was the ghost tied in to this mystery after all?

"At least the lighthouse is locked, so the ghost can't get in," George said.

Nancy thought that ghosts might be able to pass through locked doors, but she didn't mention it. She just hoped for the best.

Nancy crept down the final two stairs and fumbled to get the key in the lock. The key fit! Nancy turned it one way and the door unlocked. She turned it again and the door locked with a satisfying click. Behind her, George drew a sigh of relief.

Then George pointed to a spot above the lock. "A peephole!" she said. "Want to look?"

Nancy shook her head. She didn't want to admit it, but she was pretty scared. George was feeling brave, though, and she said, "Well, I've never seen a ghost before. I'm going to take a peek."

George stood on her tiptoes and put her eye to the peephole. Nancy was afraid to ask, but she had to. "What does it look like?" she croaked.

George's face broke into a smile as she said, "That ghost looks just like Hayley Meaney!" She reached for the lock, twisted the key in it again, and threw open the door. Hayley stood a few feet away, wailing with all her might into what looked like a megaphone.

George shouted, "What do you think you're doing?"

Hayley looked at George and crumpled onto the sandy ground. "I'm tired of being left out! Megan ignores me every summer. I thought it would be better this year, but it isn't!" With that, Hayley collapsed into tears.

Nancy didn't know what to do with her. But soon she had another problem on her

hands. Now Megan was at the bottom of the stairs, saying, "I thought I'd come down here to see if you guys needed any help!" Nancy thought that Megan might take care of her sister. But instead Megan reached for the key, which was still in the lock. "I think I can solve your mystery now. This is Abigail's key to the lighthouse."

Nancy had figured that out already, but she still had a couple of questions. "Is this how Abigail used to get up here on her own?" she asked Megan.

"I think so," Megan said, a little less boldly than usual.

"Didn't you come up here with her all the time?" Nancy wondered.

"At least once," Megan mumbled. "We had a sleepover."

Nancy felt like she was missing something. "If you thought Abigail had a key, why didn't you tell us? She mentioned a key in her note. You must have known right away what she meant!"

Megan looked at the ground. "I wasn't sure she meant that key," she insisted. "And if she did, I thought I might be able to find it myself. I'd love to have a key to this lighthouse! It's peaceful and quiet here—and my sister can't get in. Lucky I found that ladder this year. I've been going in all week."

Nancy still didn't understand. "But if you wanted Abigail's key to the lighthouse, why didn't you just ask her for it? She was moving. She didn't need it."

Megan Meaney looked embarrassed. "The last couple of summers, we didn't see each other that much. . . ." Megan trailed off, and Nancy knew what she was saying. She and Abigail weren't really friends anymore, in spite of what Megan had said. Bess and George were right.

Nancy felt a little sorry for Megan. She wanted to be nice to her. "Why did you tell us she was your best friend, then?" she asked quietly.

Megan was practically whispering now. "I just want to feel I belong here, like she did. It's my favorite place in the world! And I can't believe we have to go home at the end of the week. . . ." Megan's voice broke. Then she finally noticed her sister.

"Is this the 'ghost'?" she asked slowly.

Hayley nodded through her tears, and Megan looked shocked.

"But why were you haunting us?" Megan asked.

"I just wanted to spend some time with you this year. You're always off with your friends!" Hayley cried. "Or off on your own, I guess. I can't believe you were hiding from me!"

Now it was Megan's turn to feel bad. "I'm sorry, Hayley! I just can't stand the way you copy me!"

"I'm sorry I scared you," Hayley said, wiping her nose. "But you did pay attention, for once!"

Nancy wanted to say something about how there were better ways to get attention. But Megan could handle her sister herself. She gave Hayley a bear hug.

Then suddenly Nancy saw another face behind Megan's. Bess had made it down the stairs in one piece. Nancy thought Bess would be mad at Hayley. But instead she still seemed worried. Bess looked at Nancy and said, "Your dad doesn't know we're here. And it's dark!"

None of the girls had noticed the last of the daylight fading. Awkwardly they rushed back to the B and B together. Nancy was glad they had solved the mystery, but she wished she didn't know so much about Megan and Hayley now. She hated to hear about sisters who didn't get along.

Mr. Drew spotted the girls from the deck and raced down to meet them. "Thank goodness!" he said. "I was about to call the ice cream parlor!" Nancy hugged her dad and excused herself for a minute. She and her friends had to have another meeting upstairs.

George couldn't resist teasing Bess. "So your ghost turned out to be a little girl," she said.

But Bess couldn't resist teasing Nancy. "I knew there was something strange about Megan Meaney, even when you tried to make friends."

Nancy stood up for Megan. "Megan was doing what any of us might do. She wanted to belong here. She just made a few mistakes."

"Like avoiding her sister, not telling us about the key, and pretending Abigail was her best friend when she wasn't. Does that about cover it?" George wanted to know.

Nancy smiled and ignored George's question. "We know what the key is now, and that's enough. Now I have an idea. We don't want to treat Megan like she treated us, right?"

Bess and George looked curious about where this was going. "No . . . ," they said in unison.

"Or treat Megan the way she treated her sister?" Nancy continued.

"No . . . ," they said again.

"So how about we invite her and Hayley to sleep over here tonight? We have an extra space in that bunk bed and an extra sleeping bag—thanks to Bess!" Nancy said. "And while we're not in the lighthouse, we're about as close as we can get."

"You are too nice, Nancy Drew," Bess said after a minute. "But I guess it's the right thing to do."

"Great!" said Nancy happily. "And let's leave the key with Mrs. Webb. Maybe she can take other kids inside."

Bess and George were ready to go downstairs, but Nancy waved them ahead of her. "I'll be right there," she said. "I'll find you wherever Megan is." When the door closed behind them, Nancy took out her notebook. And before she joined her friends, she scribbled a few more things in it:

I knew Megan wasn't a meanie, in spite of her name. But her sister sure thought she was! The key to our mystery was a key to the lighthouse. And we'll make sure the light shines for all kids who come to the Webbs' in the future.

Case closed!